Published in Singapore by Epigram Books
www.epigrambooks.sg

National Library Board Singapore
Cataloguing-in-Publication Data

Phua, San San.
The very solid adventures of Handsome Hock and Champion Poh/
Phua San San. – Singapore : Epigram Books, c2013.
p. cm.
ISBN : 978-981-07-5585-0 (pbk.)
1. Boys – Juvenile fiction. 2. Friendship – Juvenile fiction.
3. Singapore – Juvenile fiction. I. Title.

PZ7
S823 – dc23   OCN829353812

First Edition 10 9 8 7 6 5 4 3 2 1

THE VERY SOLID ADVENTURES OF HANDSOME HOCK AND CHAMPION POH

PHUA SAN SAN

EPIGRAM BOOKS / SINGAPORE

This book is dedicated to my Pa for his fighting spirit, my Ma for always smiling, and to Sha, for being the best sister ever. And to Dick Lim, for being friends at first sight.

CONTENTS

FRIENDS AT FIRST SIGHT

In Singapore, not too long ago,
somewhere in the heart of Toa Payoh
on different floors of the same flat
lived two boys who had not met.

Tan Lye Hock was one boy's name,
but he thought it was a bit mundane.
He said, "I am quite a handsome chap,
even though my teeth have gaps.

"With other boys if you compare,
I have very *stylo-mylo* hair.
Watch me comb it into a *curry-pok*.
So, call me Handsome, Handsome Hock."

The other boy, he was never slow.
Everything was go-go-go!
He was faster on his feet,
than any seven-year-old you'd meet.

When he won his first race at one,
the proud father said to his son:
"You are fast in every way,
we'll call you Champion from today."

The boys were seven when they first met
at a chance encounter, just like that.
When at the playground one afternoon
Handsome was bullied by *sumseng* Boon.

Champion saw and thought it was unfair
that Boon started a fight because of a stare.
Boon was a bully, quite big for his age
but how smart he was no one could gauge.

Boon's foot stepped on Handsome's arm.
Though it hurt, Handsome Hock kept calm.
Fearing that Boon would use all his might
Champion decided to do what was right.

"Stop!" shouted Champion, "*Oi*! Let go!"
"WHO YOU?" asked Boon, "Don't *kay-poh*!"
He reached for Champion, about to smack,
but Champion ducked and dodged the attack.

Champion was fast and Champion was quick.
He made Boon dizzy with his high-speed trick.
Handsome saw the chance and wriggled free.
"Come back here, you two!" Boon said angrily.

Champion pointed, "Look, your mother!" he lied.
Boon turned to look, scared enough to hide.
The two boys ran as fast as they could.
With the bully far behind them, all was good.

Handsome said thank you, and rubbed his sore arm.
Champion even gave him some white Tiger Balm.
Handsome looked at Champion and shook his hand.
It was friends at first sight for the two young men.

The two boys can talk and play all day,
close like brothers, some would say.
Handsome Hock and Champion Poh,
they are best friends in Toa Payoh.

HOW TO CURRY-POK

We Wish For Fish

The two boys, after school each day
would head to the playground or park to play.
After that they liked to make a stop
at Uncle Bun's wonderful Lucky Cake Shop.

The shop was filled with delicious things:
cakes, cookies, bread, and buns with red beans.
Uncle Bun was nice, and a hardworking man
and the boys often offered him a helping hand.

They helped him deliver orders of bread
or poured *kaya* into glass bottles instead.
In return Uncle Bun would give the boys a treat,
sometimes a slice of cake or bread to eat.

As for bits and pieces too small to sell
the boys had an idea to use them well.
Said Uncle Bun, "You can do as you wish."
Cheered the boys, "Yay, let's go feed the fish!"

In the park was a pond next to a big tree
and in it were fish swimming with glee.
These were two boys the fish liked to greet
for they always brought food for them to eat.

Red fish, white fish, black, orange and grey
sloshed, swam and wiggled in their own fishy way.
Said Champion, "I would like fish in my home."
Said Handsome, "Let's get some of our own!"

Two boys in a pet shop with a thousand fish,
to own some was their greatest wish.
"These fish are not cheap," they said as they gazed
at tanks of guppies and angel fish, amazed.

The boys were about to give up; they were upset,
when in the shop, Handsome saw a large fish net
for two dollars fifty, which was a good deal
because in the pond, there were free fish to steal!

The boys started work to earn enough for the net.
Each errand for a neighbour, a few cents they'd get.
They worked very hard for three months, more or less,
and then the net was theirs! Hooray! Success!

Handsome proudly held the net and Champion a pail.
The pond was full of fish, no way they could fail!
When the net went in, chased some fish swimming,
a voice shouted, "STOP! What are you doing?"

A man in a uniform, his fist in the air
 ran towards them calling, "You boys over there!"
"Trouble!" said Champion, "We don't want to be caught!"
 The boys dashed away, dropped the net they had bought.

With no fish, no net, feeling sorry as well,
 they were back at the cake shop with a tale to tell.
"It's wrong to steal," said Uncle Bun, after their story.
 The boys said, "We know now, and we're sorry."

Uncle Bun knew the boys worked hard for the net,
now both had nothing…except for regret.
He took a cake box, which he cut and trimmed
into a fish tank, and stuck paper fish in.

Now the two boys, after school for the day
had something they could not wait to play.
It was a special fish tank that they liked a lot
made by wonderful Uncle from the Lucky Cake Shop.

INCIDENT REPORT

Date: 19 June 1972
Location: Park A, near Toa Payoh, Street 5
Made by: Lim Yew Ling, Assistant Park Administrator
Title: Illegal fishing by minors

Today, at approximately 3pm, I saw two young boys at the fish pond at the park. The boys were seven or eight years old. They were acting suspiciously at the edge of the pond. As I got closer, I noticed that they had a long fish net and a pail. One boy had the net in the water as the other boy held the pail.

When I shouted at them, they dropped the net and the pail and ran very fast. They disappeared quickly behind the trees and shrubs. I believe they did not take any fish with them. No park property was damaged or stolen.

Their fish net looked brand-new and has been confiscated by me since they probably will not be coming to collect it. The net is now in the park office, and is used by the park attendants as it is a good net—very strong. The pail is used to collect water leaking from the ceiling in the office when it rains.

I have alerted all the attendants at the park to look out for these two boys in case they try to steal fish again. One of the attendants said that the two boys are nice boys, as they always bring bread crumbs to feed the fish. On account that the two boys were probably too young to know what they were doing, I have not pursued the matter.

Action to be taken:
None.

PARK OFFICER

WHAT MILO
CAN DO FOR YOU

Waiting indoors for the rain to stop
the two boys drank Milo, first iced, then hot.
At last the raindrops fell very slow.
Said Champion to Handsome, "Let's go-go-go!"

Off to the playground, into puddles they leapt;
drops of water flew, with each stomping step.
They folded boats with paper they found,
in a puddle the boats could only go round.

A big and long drain was not far from home,
the big *longkang*, that's how it was known.
After the rain, the water level rose high,
perfect for a boat race, the boys had to try.

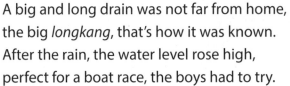

One-two-three-GO! The boats went at high speed.
The boys followed along, very thrilled indeed.
Just then a slipper drifted by and overtook their boats,
followed by a little girl who could hardly keep afloat!

"Help!" yelled the girl, struggling in the water.
Said the boys, "We must try to help her!"
They looked around for a stick or a pole
long enough to reach and let the girl hold.

No one else could help, but they found rope nearby
so they went to a tree, with one end to tie.
When it was secure, they took the other end,
and threw it close to the little girl's hand.

She grabbed the rope, but the current was strong.
It looked like she couldn't hold on for long.
Said Handsome, who did not have a plan,
"Run for help, Champion, run as fast as you can!"

Handsome himself went into the water.
The current was strong, but he was stronger.
The girl was scared though her eyes filled with hope
as Handsome moved closer, one hand on the rope.

He reached her and said, "Grab hold of me!
Don't worry, *mei mei*, just hold on tightly!"
He wrapped the rope twice around his hand
and hoped he would soon set eyes on his friend.

As soon as he wished, shouted a voice he knew,
"Hang on, Handsome, I've come back for you!"
Champion brought help, a group of men
to rescue the girl and her brave new friend.

Handsome and Champion were relieved to see
the little girl reunited with her family.
When her father thanked them, all they could say
was, "Uncle, it's because we had two Milos today."

When they refused Uncle's money, he gave instead
two brand new toy boats, one blue and one red.
And to add on to the two boys' cheer,
Uncle bought them each enough Milo to last a year.

HOW TO FOLD
A PAPER BOAT

1

2

3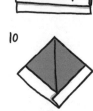

4

5

6

7

8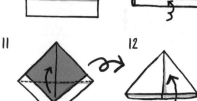

9

10

11

12

13

14

15

16

BRUCE LEE GOES TO JURONG

Talcum powder was everywhere
on Handsome's face, neck and underwear.
He put on his best T-shirt and shorts.
"Wah, so *lang zai*!" Handsome thought.

Handsome wanted to look just right
because Pa was taking them out tonight.
Their family was off to watch a movie;
it was Bruce Lee's new film, *Fist of Fury*!

Pa said, "Ask your friend to come along,
we're going to the cinema in Jurong."
And so Champion showed up at six o'clock
in front of the home of Handsome Hock.

In the back of Pa's pick-up truck,
the two boys enjoyed their good luck.
Laughing as they sat side by side,
enjoying the wind and the scenic ride.

They drove in to the largest drive-in
that Singaporeans had ever seen.
Hundreds of cars filled the open space,
from near and far they had driven to this place.

A giant screen stretched across the parking lot.
Pa drove around till he found the perfect spot.
The grown-ups paid two dollars a movie,
while the kids under twelve cost a dollar only.

To hear the film, Pa got a speaker,
then went to get snacks and food for dinner.
He was back with four Coney dogs from A&W,
kachang puteh and Kickapoo too!

Handsome and Champion gobbled everything up;
what a treat to eat in the back of Pa's pick-up.
On cardboard sheets they sat cross-legged.
Soon the screen came alive, the movie started!

Bruce Lee punched, yelled and kicked
all the bad guys who thought he was weak.
He moved so fast they could hardly see
how he completely defeated each enemy.

The two boys totally loved the show,
and declared Bruce Lee their brand-new hero.
Now all Handsome and Champion wanted to do
was to practise some powerful kung fu!

On the windy ride back, the boys fell asleep;
tired from excitement, there was hardly a peep.
Handsome and Champion's faces each had a smile
as they dreamt of fighting…Bruce Lee style!

The yummy scent that filled the air
reached his nose before he got there.
Champion's delicious dinner treat
smelled of charcoal fire roasting meat.

He soon saw an open space,
a breezy, balmy tree-filled place.
Under pointed roofs was seated a crowd.
The food was plenty, the laughter loud.

His father said, "The food's *sedap*!
Tonight we eat at the Satay Club!"
Champion's parents quickly found a seat.
Then Pa went off to get food to eat.

He ordered from Fatman's Stall Number One,
where many waited for their satay to be done.
On a charcoal pit with orange flames teasing
satay was grilled and flipped till perfect for eating.

The satay arrived, all hot and shiny,
sticks of meat served with peanut gravy.
Three choices—chicken, beef and mutton—
to eat with slices of cucumber and onion.

The tender meat was sweet at first bite,
the burnt bits were an extra delight.
Then on the stick came the nice fatty chunk,
that would go into the gravy for an extra dunk.

On the plate was another favourite part,
the rice-filled packets…mmm, *ketupat*!
Into smaller cubes Pa cut them up,
Champion dipped them into the gravy cup.

The food was tasty, the three ate fast.
Pa ordered more for the enjoyment to last.
Champion chewed and munched with delight
eating with his parents in the evening light.

When the satay man came to collect his fee
he gathered the sticks for all to see.
He counted the sticks at ten cents each.
The total? They had eaten sixty-six!

Pa said, "Now we finish our *makan*,
shall we go *jalan-jalan*?"
To end the night they took a stroll,
looked at the sea, and saw waves roll.

Strolling along Queen Elizabeth Walk,
hearing families and couples laugh and talk.
For Champion this evening was extra-sweet;
being with Ma and Pa, his joy was complete.

Handsome raised his arm to throw
the ball at someone moving slow.
Hantam Bola was the name
of this rather violent childhood game.

When Lady Luck was not with you,
you could get hit till black-and-blue.
But these ten boys loved it all the same,
the fun part was to avoid the pain.

Handsome's throw, it failed to stun;
the ball was now on the run.
Champion chased, it was his turn to throw
but *aiyoh*! It went where it shouldn't go.

A tall teen joined the group of boys.
"I WANT TO PLAY!" he said with a loud voice.
He had the ball, and gripped it tightly.
It was *sumseng* Boon, the big mean bully.

Boon's ball hit a boy who just stood there.
Handsome was angry. "Hey, that's not fair!"
Replied Boon, "HA! Then RUN, *lor*, RUN!"
Everyone ran, there was no more fun.

Boon was strong and mean indeed,
he threw the ball with force and speed.
No one had a chance to get the ball,
sumseng Boon snatched the ball from all.

Soon the ten boys were getting bruised,
one boy even had a tooth knocked loose.
" *Sumseng* Boon must be stopped,
or my name is not Handsome Hock!"

Handsome told Champion of his plan
and got everyone to understand
what all of them were about to do
to the bully, and to wait for his cue.

"Boon!" he said. "We change the game!
A special hide-and-seek, with money to gain.
If you find us, we give you ten cents each,
so if you *pasang*, you can get rich."

"Count to a hundred, and in ten minutes
you must find all ten of us before you quit!"
Boon's eyes gleamed; he could not wait to play
and get money from all the boys that day.

Boon turned around and closed his eyes,
"Start! One…two…three…four…five…."
Each boy ran home and was safe behind a door
before Boon could count to twenty-four!

DRINKING
ANG MO TEH

"Good morning!" said form teacher Mrs Lee.
"Good morning Mrs Leeeee," mumbled Class 2B.
She said, "A new student joins our class today,
please welcome Alexander Colin Hathaway."

The new student at the front of the class
had gold hair and eyes like blue glass.
A thousand small dots were on his pale skin;
his face wasn't round, it was long and thin.

"Hello," said Alexander Colin Hathaway.
"Do call me Alex. Pleased to meet you today."
Alex spoke perfect English, the kind you hear on TV.
He said, "I come from England, the land of jam and tea."

The class was restless as they watched the clock.
Once it rang for recess, they all wanted to talk.
Around Alex they stood, a little shy at first;
then the questions came in a noisy burst.

"Are you wearing a wig? Are you *ang moh*?"
There was a lot that his classmates wanted to know.
"Why you talk like that? Do you find the weather hot?"
"Do you like durians? How many dots your skin got?"

Alex had answers, but he came to a stop,
stunned by the hairstyle of Handsome Hock.
Impressed, he said, "That's splendid, old chap!
Will you teach me how to make my hair like that?"

Handsome was puzzled. "Old? Is 'splandeed' good?"
So Alex explained what had not been understood.
"Splendid is very good, and old chap is a friend.
Pleased to meet you," he said, and stuck out his hand.

Handsome shook his hand. "I am Handsome Hock.
Our English is different, I teach you so we can talk.
'Splendid' is solid and 'old chap' is *peng you*.
'Pretty girl' is *lang looi*, *lang zai* is us two."

"Someone too excited is called *kancheong* spider,
but he is *boh chup*, if everything doesn't matter.
Marbles are *go-lee*, and coffee is *kopi*,
fried noodles are *char mee*, and bread is called *roti*."

Alex learned fast and Handsome was impressed.
"We'll call you Ah Lek, it means clever and the best!"
Ah Lek was invited to join his classmates' adventures,
soon he felt at home, and the days passed like hours.

In March, for his birthday, Alex asked Mrs Lee
if he could bring in some jam biscuits, cake and tea.
While everyone sipped from teacups and ate,
he read a poem he wrote for his class of thirty-eight.

" My heart leaps up when I behold a rainbow in the sky.
 I really like durians, *prata*, ice *kachang* and *chap chye*.
 Kam siah for being a *peng you* to this simple English boy,
 I will never forget all of you, and *gung hei fatt choy*."

Mrs Lee was speechless as the class clapped their hands.
" Magnificent! Smashing!" they praised their English friend.
 Alex took a bow, combed his hair into a *curry-pok*.
" That's brilliant, old chap!" said a proud Handsome Hock.

Handsome cut and pasted, and coloured very hard,
he was making a handsome heart-shaped card.
In his best handwriting, he wrote "Thank you, Ma" in pink,
signed off "Your handsome son, Ah Hock" in purple ink.

Mother's Day was Sunday and he could not wait,
for Ma to see the card he had specially made.
He hid the card in his schoolbag, ran home excited.
But when he got home, Ma was not delighted.

"Ah Hock, why so late!" she said. "Your lunch is cold!
Put your dirty shoes where you have been told!"
No chance to interrupt at all, his mother did not stop.
There was no escape for poor Handsome Hock.

She was in a bad mood, he did not know why.
He ate his lunch in silence with a quiet sigh.
"Do your homework!" she said. "Don't only play-play!
Waste time like that, you will never get an A!"

Ah Hock felt angry, and then he felt quite sad.
Was he such a lousy son, so stupid and so bad?
In his room he took out the card he made that day,
crumpled it into a tiny ball and threw it away.

When Ma was cooking dinner, he slipped out the door,
"I don't want to be home, Ma doesn't like me any more."
That was what he thought as he walked out feeling blue,
he was sad and sorry and did not know what to do.

He walked to the big *longkang*, and at his favourite spot,
sat then laid down; he slept for quite a lot.
When he woke it was dark, no lamps lit up the place,
Handsome was a brave boy, but fear was on his face.

He wanted to be home now, but first he had to find,
a way home but with no light, he was almost blind.
He walked into *lalang*, which scratched his skin.
Ow! He tripped and fell, hit his forehead and shin.

Handsome hobbled and he limped in pain.
To make matters worse, it began to rain.
He had never felt so miserable, cold, and hungry as well.
Then he heard a voice… "Handsome Hock!" it yelled.

Handsome was found by his friend Champion Poh,
because he knew where Handsome liked to go.
The two made their way to where Handsome's parents waited;
they saw his bloodied face and arms and almost fainted.

With tears in her eyes, Handsome's ma hugged him tightly.
"Why you frighten Ma like that?" she asked softly.
"Pa lost his job today, I didn't know what to do.
Ma loves you, Ah Hock, I'm sorry I shouted at you."

Though covered with plasters, Handsome felt no pain.
He wanted to do his best to make Ma happy again.
He told himself to study hard and make his parents proud,
earn a lot of money, and stand out from the crowd.

Once home, he could not find the card he'd thrown away,
in it was his message to Ma for Mother's Day.
But to his delight he spied something familiar—
Ma had found his card and put it on the refrigerator.

Handsome was stressed and confused.
"How come English so difficult to use?"
Alex said, "Don't worry, I'll help you cram.
You will pass your English exam!"

Handsome had only two weeks left to go,
for English Language, his score was low.
Spelling was okay for words that were easy,
Handsome could spell A-P-P-L-E.

Longer words he could not spell well,
'bicycle' came out as B-Y-S-I-K-E-L.
Alex gave him some friendly advice:
"For spelling, the secret is to MEMORISE!"

Handsome wished time would not disturb
and transform the spelling of a verb.
How 'go' became 'went' did not make sense
just because one was present and the other, past tense.

"Verbs are funny creatures," Alex tried to explain.
"Some change the same way, some don't play the game.
 Keep using them, practise, and never fear,
 if you use them enough, you will develop an ear."

So Handsome listened, read and memorised.
No extra ear grew, no words appeared before his eyes.
While using his eraser, he had a desperate plan:
his eraser could give him a helping hand.

In the smallest handwriting he could write
he wrote verbs that he could never get right.
Words he could not spell also took a place,
on the eraser he would put into his pencil case.

On the morning of his English exam,
his Pa said to him, "I'm proud of you, young man.
Whatever you score, you have done your best.
You've studied hard, Pa is impressed."

At the school hall, Alex also came to say,
"Good luck! You've worked hard for this day!"
Handsome was ashamed of his dishonest plan.
He said, "I'll use my own effort to take this exam!"

He threw away the eraser before he entered the hall.
The questions were easy! He could answer almost all!
Studying had done him some good.
At the end of the exam, he was in a happy mood.

The exam paper reads:

ENGLISH EXAM
Name: Tan Lye Hock   75/100
Class: 2B

Please answer the following questions:
1. Susan is riding a bicycle.
2. She is a student in the school.
3. She goes to school everyday. She goes to school daily.
4. She likes school. She is happy.

Handsome passed! And his score was high!
Upon a hundred marks, he got 75!
"Thank you, Alex, for making my English powderful!"
Alex laughed and said, "The power was from you!"

PA AND UNCLE PETER LOW

Champion's Pa had many friends
but none could be more welcome than
the friendly Uncle Peter Low
who liked to visit him in Toa Payoh.

Uncle Peter was tan and tall.
In his booming voice, he would call,
"POH! It's PETER! How are YOU?"
Pa always said, "GOOD, my old *peng you*!"

These two friends liked to talk and laugh.
Of each other they never had enough.
Uncle Peter was at their house today
when Handsome Hock came to play.

The boys asked him to tell a tale
and that, Uncle Peter, would never fail.
He said, "Have you heard of the flying fox?
Or how I survived four electric shocks?"

From shooting tigers to crocodiles,
to walking for two hundred miles,
Uncle Peter's life was like taking a look
through colourful pages of a storybook.

He said, "Life can be a fantastic dream
and take you to many strange extremes.
But no matter where life brings you to,
remember the people who care for you.

When I was young and poor and weak,
your Pa saved me, gave me food to eat.
Though we were poor, we did not cheat.
We worked very hard to make ends meet."

They sold noodles and carried bricks,
ate leftovers and made satay sticks.
For more than twenty years did Pa and Peter
go through thick and thin together.

"Your Pa and me, we became good friends
from the moment he gave me a helping hand."
This was how Champion and Handsome knew
about the way this faithful friendship grew.

That night, Champion told Handsome Hock,
" We will grow up, but our friendship won't stop.
You, Handsome Hock and me, Champion Poh,
will be just like Pa and Uncle Peter Low."

⭐ Special words ⭐⭐
by Handsome Hock

1. Solid - means very very very good.
2. Stylo-mylo - smart and handsome
3. Peng You - friend (like champion and me)
4. Kam Siah - Thank you (in Hokkien)
5. Jalan-jalan - walk-walk (malay)
6. ang moh - Westerner (pa say it means someone with red hair.)
7. sum Seng - big bully, gangster (Boon ←don't like him)
8. Kay-poh - busybody, nosy